This book belongs to

_____

Published by Scholastic Inc., 90 Old Sherman Turnpike, Danbury, Connecticut 06816.

ISBN 13: 978-0-439-90226-7

ISBN 10: 0-439-90226-6

Printed in the U.S.A.

First Scholastic printing, January 2008

LarryBoy meets COLONEL CORNCOB

A Lesson in Being Content with What You Have

by **Jesse Leon McCann**

Illustrated by **Tom Bancroft** and **Rob Corley**

Colored by Jon Conkling

SCHOLASTIC INC.

New York Toronto London Auckland Sydney
Mexico City New Delhi Hong Kong Buenos Aires

Laura Carrot went out bright and early to collect old gum wrappers for her scrapbook. She spotted a very pretty gum wrapper in Bumblyburg Park and reached for it. But a stranger **snatched** the wrapper instead! "Mine!" muttered the stranger. "And it isn't enough. I must have more!"

LAURA'S GUM WRAPPERS

"Here's one—and another—and another,"
said the stranger, hopping and skipping through
the park. He quickly grabbed all the gum
wrappers, leaving none for Laura.

"It isn't fair to take them all!" Laura yelled.
"Can't you share?"

"No, no, all for me," he said. "I need lots
of things!"

The stranger **whisked** through town, collecting things. **Flash!**
He grabbed all the rubber bands on the sidewalk, a No Parking sign
from Walnut Street, and discarded ketchup packages in front the
hamburger stand! **Swish!** He took free bank deposit envelopes,
pushpins, and free Bumblyburg Online discs from the computer store!

Junior Asparagus was about to buy some goldfish, but the stranger bought them first. **Zow!** The stranger **nabbed** sand from the kindergarten sandbox, daisies from Ma and Pa Grape's flower bed, and Popsicle sticks. **Swoosh!** The stranger even took the corner fire hydrant!

Luckily, LarryBoy was on the case! He *zoomed* into Bumblyburg. As he was motoring through town, the dashboard monitor clicked on. It was Alfred.

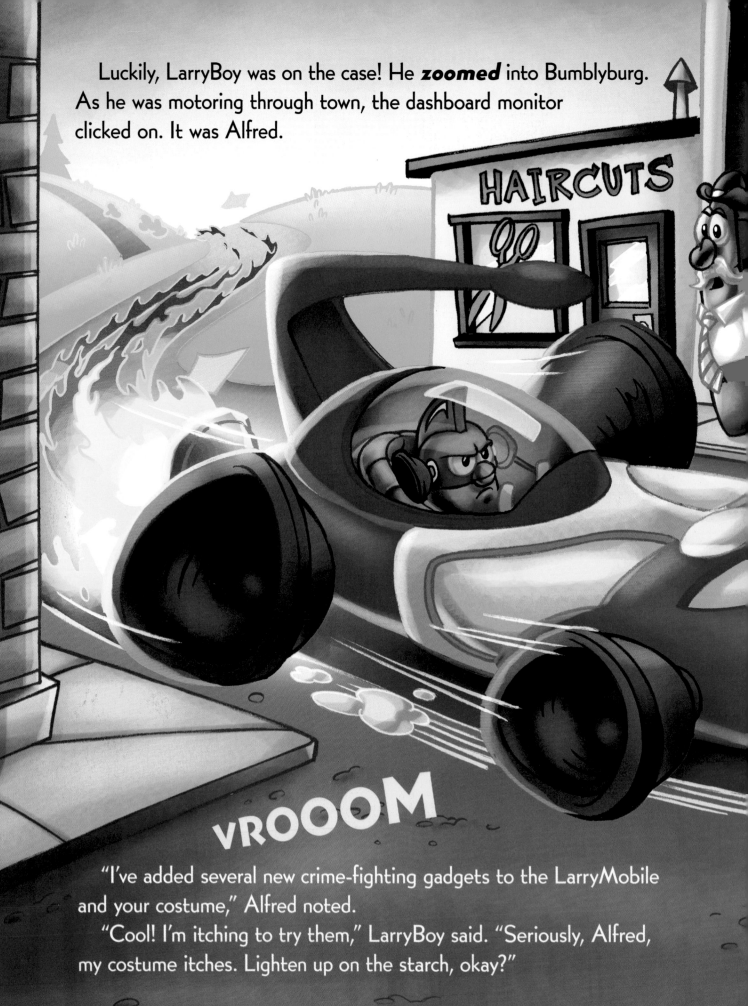

VROOOM

"I've added several new crime-fighting gadgets to the LarryMobile and your costume," Alfred noted.

"Cool! I'm itching to try them," LarryBoy said. "Seriously, Alfred, my costume itches. Lighten up on the starch, okay?"

"Please be careful with your new gadgets, Master Larry," said Alfred. "Don't ruin them right away, like you usually do!"

"Sorry, Alfred, I make no promises," LarryBoy said seriously. "A hero's gotta do what a hero's gotta do!"

LarryBoy finally spied the stranger at the Bumblyburg Ice Cream Shop, buying all sorts of things.

"Cones and spoons!" the stranger muttered. "Straws and cups and napkins! Dishes and scoops and containers and chairs! But I need more, more, **more!**"

"I have the stranger's computer file, Master Larry," Alfred said. "Oh no! He's—the **Colonel**."

"You mean the fried chicken guy?" asked LarryBoy.

"No, Colonel Corncob," Alfred said. "He's notorious for collecting things until there's nothing left to collect!"

"Not if I have anything to say about it!" LarryBoy said. He then pushed a button and fired the LarryNet, one of Alfred's new gadgets. **Sproing!** The LarryNet was sure to capture the Colonel!

Instead, Colonel Corncob quickly snagged the LarryNet with his walking stick and spun it around and around! LarryBoy went spinning, too!

WHIRRR!

"One big net—but, there's just one," said the Colonel. "One is not enough! I'll need more—from fishing boats, soccer fields, and basketball hoops! Nets, nets, and more nets. That's what I want. Nets!"

LarryBoy was sick from all the spinning. "Oooh! I'll never ride a merry-go-round again!" he moaned.

WHIRRR!

MAIL

MARSHMALLOWS

LarryBoy let go of the LarryNet and flew high into the air. Luckily, he landed on top of a big sack of marshmallows in a nearby marshmallow shop! *Moosh!*

Meanwhile, back at LarryBoy's mansion, Alfred was watching everything that was happening.

"Oh no! Master Larry, do you realize what you've done?" Alfred cried. "Colonel Corncob has added your brand-new LarryNet to his collection!"

LarryBoy couldn't understand why Alfred was upset. It wasn't LarryBoy's fault Colonel Corncob took the LarryNet. "Gee, Alfred, I would think you would be happy that I wasn't badly hurt by the fall,"

"Oh yes, of course, Master Larry, well done," Alfred added. Alfred suddenly realized he could have lost LarryBoy for good. He could always make another LarryNet.

"Master Larry, the computer has tracked Colonel Corncob to the outskirts of Bumblyburg," Alfred said, when LarryBoy returned to the LarryMobile.

"Excellent!" LarryBoy exclaimed, smiling. "He must be in his top secret, ultrahigh-tech lair, with computers and gizmos and all sorts of villain stuff!"

"Actually, it's his parents' house," said Alfred.

"Stop right there, Colonel!" LarryBoy shouted when he arrived. "You'll do no more collecting on my watch!"

"I don't have enough!" cried the Colonel. "Go away! I need more. Go away!"

"If you resist, I warn you—I have new hero gadgets in my costume!" LarryBoy said.

But Colonel Corncob had gadgets, too! The battle was over very quickly.

"I can't believe your gadgets are all ruined!" Alfred cried over LarryBoy's earphone. "And your freshly starched costume is all wrinkly!"

"Not now, Alfred," LarryBoy said. "I'm a little hung up at the moment."

LarryBoy decided to try a sneakier approach. If he could creep up on the Colonel, perhaps he would catch him off guard. Unfortunately, it was the Colonel who caught LarryBoy!

THOOOUP!

TRAP DOOR

ONE PHONE

"Now I have a superhero in my collection!" cheered Colonel Corncob. "Is one enough? Probably not! I need more superheroes—more, more, more."

LarryBoy landed in a big glass jar.
A giant claw screwed the lid on tight.
He was trapped, but it didn't mean
he couldn't talk some sense into
Colonel Corncob.

"Why do you need all this stuff, Colonel?" LarryBoy
asked. "It's so crowded in here that you can hardly move! Besides
that, you're making a lot of people unhappy," added LarryBoy.

For a moment, the Colonel seemed to listen to LarryBoy. "Hmmm, let me collect my thoughts," Colonel Corncob said. "You make some good points—but no, I like to collect too much!"

The Colonel seemed quite pleased with himself, until—
Ping! Pang! CRRRASH! A big wall of his collection
came tumbling down on him!

"Oww! You were right, LarryBoy—I did collect too much
stuff!" Colonel Corncob moaned.

"Don't worry, Colonel," encouraged LarryBoy. "I'll save you!"

LarryBoy straightened a paper clip to push the claw's open button. **Sherrsh! Pop!** The lid opened. "Hey, Alfred," LarryBoy smiled. "I used one of your new gadgets, and I didn't wreck it!"

"That's a paper clip," Alfred said over LarryBoy's earphone. "I use it to keep your costume on its hanger."

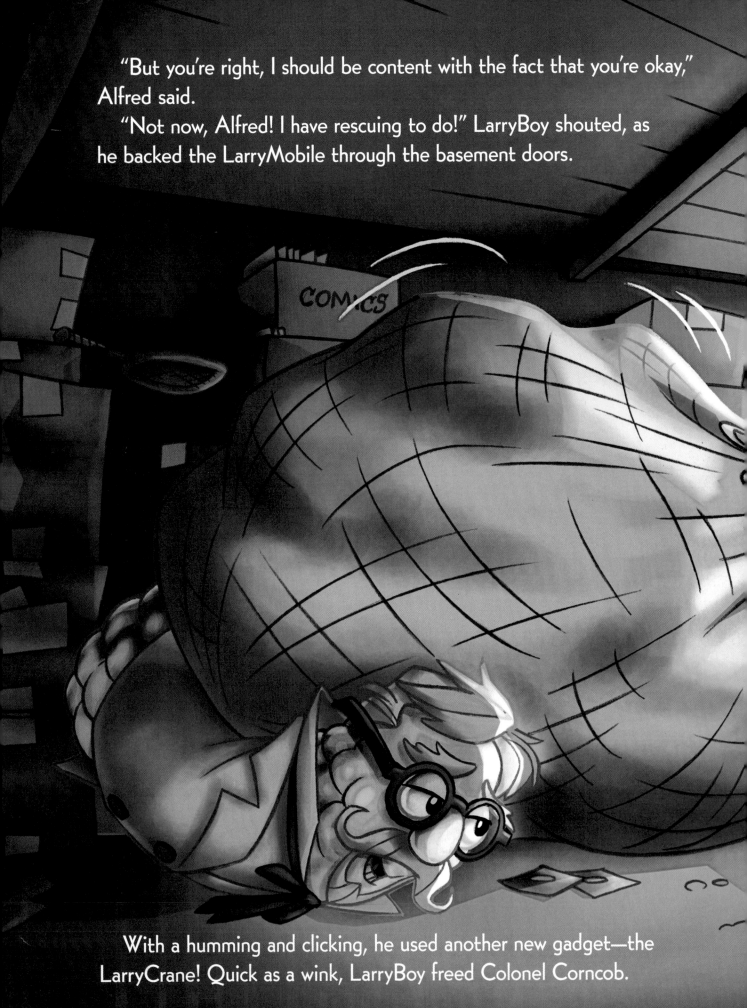

"But you're right, I should be content with the fact that you're okay," Alfred said.

"Not now, Alfred! I have rescuing to do!" LarryBoy shouted, as he backed the LarryMobile through the basement doors.

With a humming and clicking, he used another new gadget—the LarryCrane! Quick as a wink, LarryBoy freed Colonel Corncob.

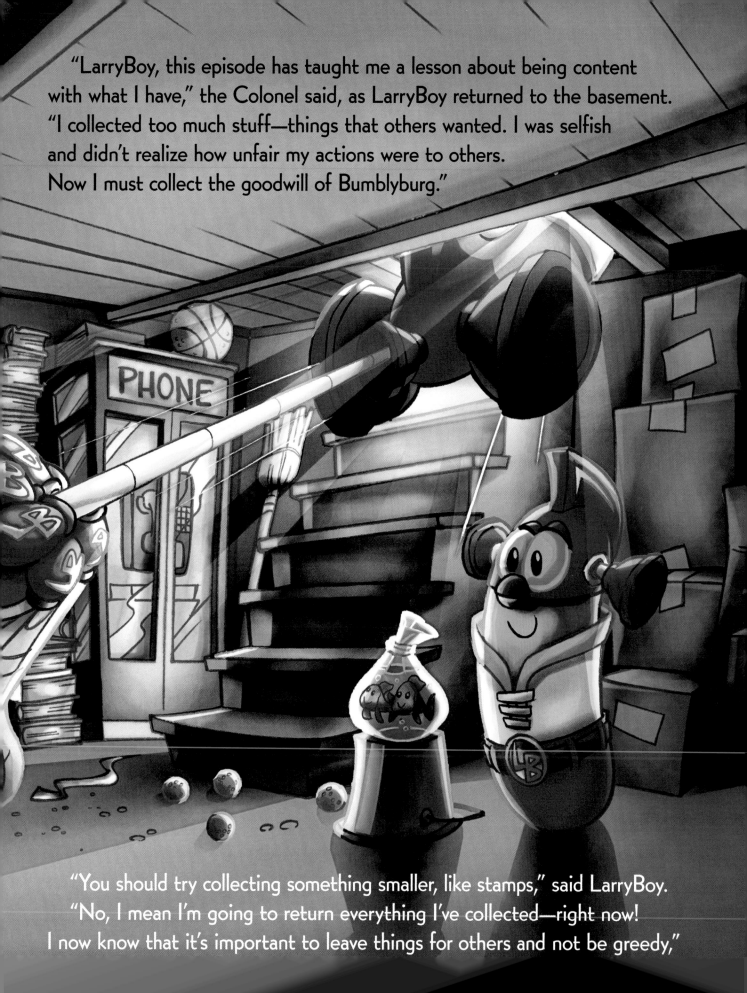

"LarryBoy, this episode has taught me a lesson about being content with what I have," the Colonel said, as LarryBoy returned to the basement. "I collected too much stuff—things that others wanted. I was selfish and didn't realize how unfair my actions were to others. Now I must collect the goodwill of Bumblyburg."

"You should try collecting something smaller, like stamps," said LarryBoy. "No, I mean I'm going to return everything I've collected—right now! I now know that it's important to leave things for others and not be greedy,"

It is better to have a little and do right
than to have a lot and be unfair.
Proverbs 16:8